By

The Little Book OF BIG WHAT-IFS

RENATA LIWSKA

HOUGHTON MIFFLIN HARCOURT
Boston   New York

To all the kind people who help clear
away my uncertainties —R.L.

hmhco.com

The text of this book is set in Caslon Twelve.
The illustrations are drawn with pencil and colored digitally.

Library of Congress Catalog Information is on file.
ISBN: 978-1-328-76701-1

Manufactured in Malaysia
TWP 10 9 8 7 6 5 4 3 2 1
4500743344

What if you slept through your birthday?

What if no one could hear you?

What if everyone could?

What if you swallowed a seed?

What if it doesn't grow?

What if there was only one way?

What if there was only one kind?

What if there were way too many?

What if you can't think of anything?

What if your imagination runs wild?

What if you get lost?

What if someone can help?

What if you make the time?

What if you had a long way to go?

What if it was worth the wait?

What if there is too much room?

What if there isn't enough?

What if you go off the beaten path?

What if you make a mistake?

What if we all work together?

What if we find one thing in common?

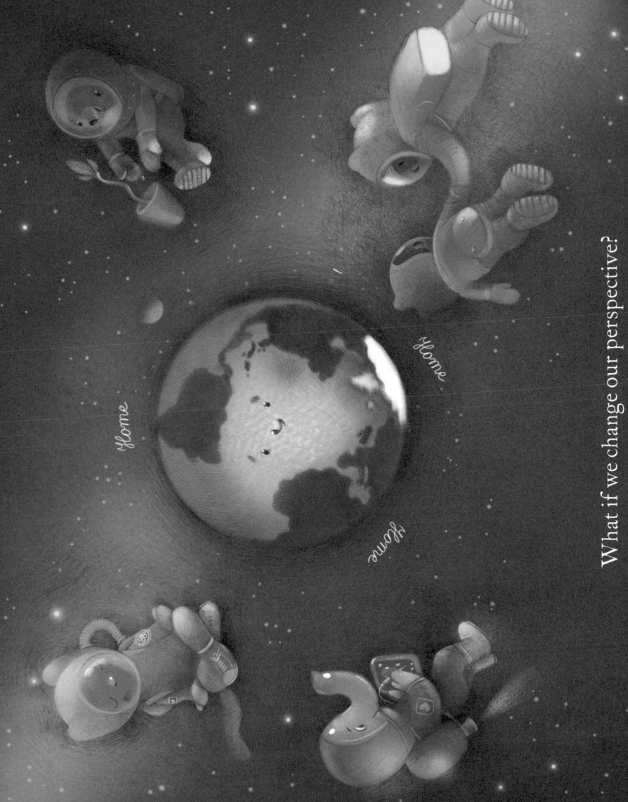

Home

Home

Home

What if we change our perspective?

What if you're surprised?

What if everyone shared?

What if it spreads?

What a difference it would make!